Parent Page

Sharing is tough. Just ask Iblis or Cain. Why can sharing be so difficult? It has something to do with pride and envy.

"I am better than [Adam]. You created me from fire, and created him from clay," Iblis petitions to Allah (SWT) in the Holy Qur'an. Before earning the name Satan, Iblis was a notable servant of Allah (SWT). However, pride, the feeling of being superior to another, led him to envy the noble status given to mankind. This pushed Iblis to disobey Allah's (SWT) command, and earn a place in the pits of hell for eternity.

Envy, or *hasad*, often results from pride. Envy is a malicious form of jealousy, in which one desires the loss of another's blessing. This vicious disease can cause individuals to commit vile actions, as demonstrated when Cain killed his brother Able (SAW). Prophet Mohammed (SAW) warns against envy, saying "Envy consumes one's faith like fire consumes wood."

So how can we protect ourselves from pride and envy? First, we must recognize the harm caused by these diseases and quell the sources. In our first story, "Vote for Me," Asad learns that envy and pride can do incredible damage, not just to himself but also to his best friend. He learns to protect himself from the negative ideas that he concocts himself, as well as from those that are relayed to him through others.

Second, we must realize that Allah's (SWT) blessings are unlimited. In the second story, "Pride and Painting," Amira begins to feel envy after another student is honored. However, she discovers that blessings from Allah (SWT) are unlimited, and that both she and her friend can be blessed. All Amira has to do is pray.

Credits
Writer: Elizabeth Lymer
Design: Annie Idris
Research: Armaan Siddiqi
Editors: Amin and Sana Aaser

Glossary
Insha'Allah
God Willing

SAW SallAllahu 'alayhi wa sallam
Peace be upon him

SWT Subhanahu wa-ta'ala
May He be glorified and exalted

It's time for the second graders at Northport Elementary to elect a President for the Student Council. It's an important role. The President decides on school lunches, picks field trips, and chooses new playground equipment.

t lunch, Shireen tries to convince Amin to run...
Remember that time when you stood up for Asad when he was being bullied by Zain?
And when you were thankful even after you had a tough day?
Jeepers, I don't know.
Asad, what do you think?
You would be an awesome President, Amin!

After Shireen and Amin leave to put away their trays, Zain arrives.

Asad thinks about what Zain said...

If Amin is elected as President of the Student Council today, then, who knows, tomorrow Amin could be Mayor of the city...

And someday, he could be President of the United States of America!

Zain is right, I'll always live in Amin's shadows...

Maybe I should run for Student Council.

Asad decides that Zain is right. He must run for Student Council and beat his best friend, Amin.

Asad waits until the hallway is clear of students, grits his teeth, and does something unlike anything he's done before. He tears down every poster, one by one, and slips them into his backpack.

Just before class, Amin sees Asad in the hallway.

Man Asad, this whole running for President thing is tough!

I just finished writing my speech. It took forever.

Asad imagines destroying his best friend's speech. He wants to ruin Amin's campaign.

After Amin leaves for class, Asad notices that Amin forgot to close his locker. And, it looks like the speech is inside!

Take the speech. Nobody will ever find out. It's your only chance...

Asad snatches Amin's paper, stuffs it into his backpack, and starts zipping it closed. When the bell rings, Asad gets up to go to class, not realizing that his backpack hasn't been fully zipped.

RRIINGG!!

While Asad is walking toward class, his backpack begins to unzip. Amin's speech and campaign posters scatter across the hallway.

Questions:

1. Does Asad normally cheat and steal? Why is Asad acting this way?
2. Is Zain a good friend or a bad friend? Should Asad listen to him?
3. Would you like to be friends with somebody who is envious?

Asad has to wait until recess to speak with Amin again. He prays silently to Allah (SWT), in between doing his classwork.

Think About It

Once upon a time, two brothers, Able and Cain, competed for the love of Allah (SWT). When Able's devotion was accepted and Cain's was not, envy took over. Cain ended up killing his own brother because of his rage.

Envy is dangerous. How could Asad have stopped himself from feeling envious of his best friend?

PRIDE and PAINTING

JazakAllah Khayran for your tour of the Art Gallery. Your works are my favorite!

Thank you, thank you.

Insha'Allah, I would love for my work to be featured here someday.

Practice your art and pray for help. That's what I did. Maybe it'll work for you too!

Just as the visitor leaves, the Art Director swings by with a surprise.

Amira, this place always needs change, doesn't it? It's a constant flow of new ideas, new people, new beauty...

Yes?

Good, I'm glad you agree. We have a new young artist joining the team! Her work is colorful and smart. You will love it.

By next weekend, Sarah's artwork is on the wall next to Amira's. Everyone who visits the gallery seems to love Sarah's work.

Sarah's Artwork

Amira's Artwork

This is my favorite piece in the whole gallery!

Doesn't everyone just love crayons?

I hope the gallery will display more pieces by this artist!

But Amira does not love crayons. She doesn't even want to look at Sarah's artwork. She feels sure her own work, with paint, is better.

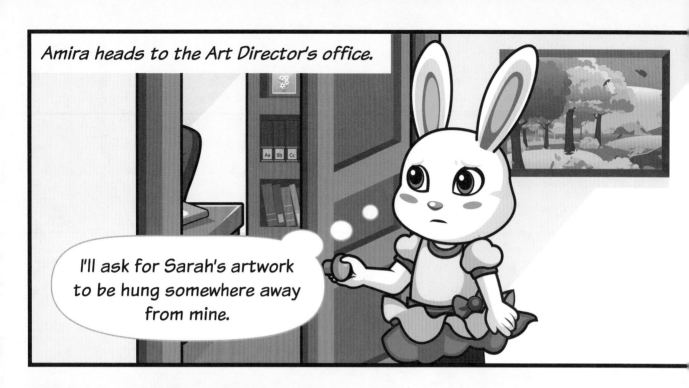

Amira heads to the Art Director's office.

I'll ask for Sarah's artwork to be hung somewhere away from mine.

A visit from the Mayor? She is searching for a new piece of artwork for City Hall? I'll have our newest team member give the tour, insha'Allah.

He must be talking about me. Sarah hasn't even started work yet. I'm the one who gives the tours.

I don't want to teach Sarah anything. I should be giving the special tour, not her!

Amira, don't let pride get the best of you. There is space at our gallery for you and Sarah.

But, my work is more elegant and detailed. Plus, crayons are for babies!

That's enough.

Sarah's work is exquisite and she deserves recognition too. You've already received so much honor, Amira. Be thankful.

Questions:

1. Is Amira acting like herself? What has gotten into her?
2. Has Allah (SWT) blessed Amira? What are examples of her blessings?
3. What will happen if Amira stays proud and does not help Sarah?

Amira is anxious. Her heart feels heavy and her body feels weak. She decides to read the Holy Qu'ran. With each verse, Amira is more at ease.

وَلاَ تَتَمَنَّوْا مَا فَضَّلَ اللهُ بِهِ بَعْضَكُمْ عَلَىٰ بَعْضٍ لِّلرِّجَالِ نَصِيبٌ مِّمَّا اكْتَسَبُوا وَلِلنِّسَاء نَصِيبٌ مِّمَّا اكْتَسَبْنَ وَاسْأَلُوا اللهَ مِن فَضْلِهِ إِنَّ اللهَ كَانَ بِكُلِّ شَيْءٍ عَلِيمًا

Do not envy the favors which God has granted to some of you. Men and women will both be rewarded according to their deeds. Instead, pray to God for His favors. (4:32)

Subhan'Allah!
I shouldn't envy Sarah.
If Allah (SWT) has blessed her,
He can bless me too.
All I have to do is pray.

The next morning, Amira arrives at the Art Gallery bright and early to help Sarah.

The next morning, Amira arrives at the Art Gallery bright and early to help Sarah.

As Salaam Alaikum. You must be Sarah!

Wa Alaikum Salaam. Yes, do you remember me?

Of course I do. It seems like all your hard work paid off!

And prayer. Lots, and lots of prayer!

Alhumdulillah. Let's get to work.

Amira teaches Sarah everything she knows about the Art Gallery. Soon the Mayor arrives and it is time for Sarah's tour.